12 Days of Christmas

we make books come alive™

pi kids® **Phoenix International Publications, Inc.**

Chicago · London · New York · Hamburg · Mexico City · Paris · Sydney

On the 1st day of Christmas
my true love gave to me
a partridge in a pear tree.

On the 2nd day of Christmas
my true love gave to me

2 turtle doves

& a partridge in a pear tree.

Kringle's Nursery was having a sale on
partridges in pear trees. But where do you
suppose my true love found two turtle
doves? (What is a turtle dove, anyway?)

MISTLETOE

BEAN STALK

SALE

PEPPERS

KRINGLE'S NURSERY

BUY YOUR
CHRISTMAS
PARTRIDGE
NOW!

PUMPKINS
$5.00
$3.00
$1.00

FREE!

FAMILY
TREE

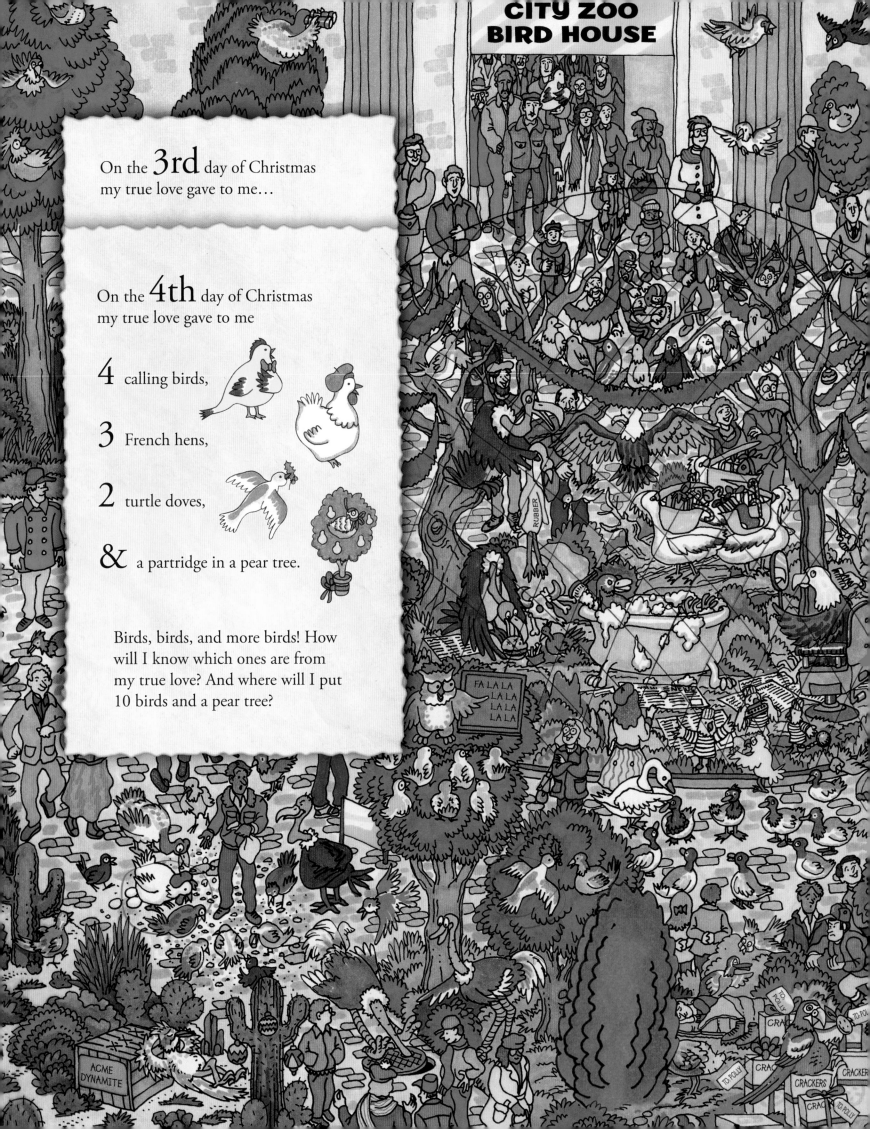

On the **3rd** day of Christmas
my true love gave to me…

On the **4th** day of Christmas
my true love gave to me

4 calling birds,

3 French hens,

2 turtle doves,

& a partridge in a pear tree.

Birds, birds, and more birds! How
will I know which ones are from
my true love? And where will I put
10 birds and a pear tree?

CITY ZOO
BIRD HOUSE

On the **5th** day of Christmas
my true love gave to me

5 golden rings,

4 calling birds,

3 French hens,

2 turtle doves,

& a partridge in a pear tree.

There's nothing like Christmas
down on the farm. It is so peaceful
and quiet. Or is it?

CHICKENS

On the **6th** day of Christmas my true love gave to me…

On the **7th** day of Christmas my true love gave to me

7 swans a-swimming,

6 geese a-laying,

5 golden rings,

4 calling birds,

3 French hens,

2 turtle doves,

& a partridge in a pear tree.

Christmas isn't all sleigh rides and snowflakes! In fact, my true love saw Santa playing a quick nine holes down in Florida this year!

On the **8th** day of Christmas
my true love gave to me

8 maids a-milking,

7 swans a-swimming,

6 geese a-laying,

5 golden rings,

4 calling birds,

3 French hens,

2 turtle doves,

& a partridge in a pear tree.

Oh, my! What shall I do with all this milk? I think I shall churn it into butter and bake cookies.

On the **9th** day of Christmas my true love gave to me

9 ladies dancing,

8 maids a-milking,

7 swans a-swimming,

6 geese a-laying,

5 golden rings,

4 calling birds,

3 French hens,

2 turtle doves,

& a partridge in a pear tree.

My true love must have had to shop around the clock to find all these swell Christmas gifts!

THE ONLY RESTAURANT WHERE YOU CAN EAT DIRT CHEAP!

GREASY SPOON WITH EVERY MEAL!

On the **10th** day of Christmas
my true love gave to me

10 lords a-leaping,

9 ladies dancing,

8 maids a-milking,

7 swans a-swimming,

6 geese a-laying,

5 golden rings,

4 calling birds,

3 French hens,

2 turtle doves,

& a partridge in a pear tree.

I'm going to need a bigger attic to hold all these lords and ladies and maids and…whew! My true love is going completely overboard this year!

PUNCH

On the **11th** day of Christmas
my true love gave to me…

On the **12th** day of Christmas
my true love gave to me

12 drummers drumming,

11 pipers piping,

10 lords a-leaping,

9 ladies dancing,

8 maids a-milking,

7 swans a-swimming,

6 geese a-laying,

5 golden rings,

4 calling birds,

3 French hens,

2 turtle doves,

& a partridge in a pear tree.

Whew! I would have been happy with a pair of mittens from my true love! Were you able to find all of the gifts on the 12 days of Christmas? If you'd like to have even more fun, go back to each scene and find these other funny things!

Kringle's Nursery

Peter Piper and his peck
of pickled peppers
George and his cherry tree
lemon that is not a fruit
two squirrels who are nuts
family tree
pumpkinhead
shoe tree

City Zoo Bird House

"A bird in the hand that's worth
more than two in the bush"
jailbirds
two cans
proud peacock
birdbath
lovebirds
even balder eagle
blackbirds baked in a pie
rubber chicken

Candy Cane Farm

The Ugly Duckling
Baa, baa, black sheep…
the farmer in the dell…
Little Bo Peep
the cow who jumped
over the moon…
Three Billy Goats Gruff
Peter, Peter, pumpkin eater…
Three Little Pigs
Little Miss Muffet
Mary who had a little lamb…

Golf Course

Santa Claus and his reindeer
hole in 1
a hero
golfer choosing an "iron"
real handlebar mustache
golf T
love at first sight
flamingo wearing golf shoes
golfer yelling "FOUR!"

Town Square

someone mailing a "card"
old man walking with
a candy cane
bird hatching ornaments
dog burying a candy cane
igloo
strange hockey stick
real stocking cap
sunbather
snow "cone" man

Soda Shop

two pairs of socks hopping
martian spaceship
hound dog
real beehive hairdo
poodle skirt barking back
customer in ice-cream shock
someone stepping on
blue-suede shoes
Santa Claus checking his menu
two bugs jitterbugging

Fancy Dress Ball

Captain Hook
guest who thinks the
punch is too strong
Rumpelstiltskin
guest dressed in fish
Cinderella's glass slipper
joker making a real toast
princess kissing a frog
The Tin Man

Christmas Parade

pied piper
scaredy-cat
three marching snowmen
elephant playing his trunk
skateboard "hotdogger"
beavers cutting a clown
down to size
purple cow
marching cupcake
half of a horse